TRANSFORMERS
EARTHSPARK

MEGATRON IS PUT TO THE TEST

adapted by Gloria Cruz

Ready-to-Read

Simon Spotlight

New York   London   Toronto   Sydney   New Delhi

SIMON SPOTLIGHT

An imprint of Simon & Schuster Children's Publishing Division
1230 Avenue of the Americas, New York, New York 10020
This Simon Spotlight edition May 2024

Simon & Schuster: Celebrating 100 Years of Publishing in 2024
For information about special discounts for bulk purchases, please contact Simon & Schuster Special Sales at 1-866-506-1949 or business@simonandschuster.com.
Manufactured in the United States of America 0424 LAK
10 9 8 7 6 5 4 3 2
ISBN 978-1-6659-5215-6 (hc)
ISBN 978-1-6659-5214-9 (pbk)
ISBN 978-1-6659-5216-3 (ebook)

Megatron has come a long way from his time as the leader of the Decepticons. He believed his purpose was to lead Transformers bots to rule the universe, and anyone who stood in his way was an enemy.

When the Decepticons lost the war to the Autobots, Megatron pledged his allegiance to Optimus Prime's vision of peace. Since then he's been a great partner to Optimus Prime.

Megatron has also been a great ally
to all humans. Sometimes he does
not understand why he has to take
orders from G.H.O.S.T., an
organization committed to the
Human–Autobot Alliance.

Megatron and Optimus Prime arrive at G.H.O.S.T. headquarters to celebrate the new Human–Autobot Alliance. Megatron is unimpressed.

Optimus Prime reminds Megatron
that they work with G.H.O.S.T. now.
He reminds Megatron it is time to
stop believing that humans think less
of Cybertronians.

Megatron is still annoyed, but he knows that Optimus Prime is right. He does stand in alliance with humans, even if he occasionally gets frustrated.

At the G.H.O.S.T. and Autobot Alliance celebration, Megatron is happy to see a few of his favorite humans, Robby, Mo, Dot, and Alex.

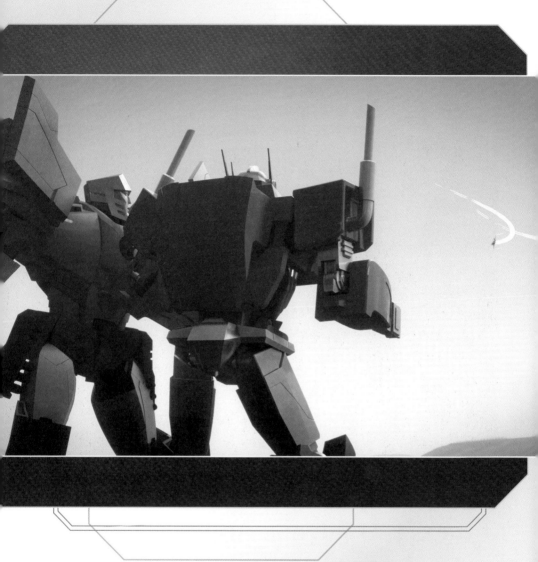

Megatron greets his friends,
but two fighter jets that are flying
very low catch his attention.

Optimus Prime and Megatron
recognize the Decepticons
Skywarp and Nova Storm, and they
warn their human allies
to run to safety.

Skywarp and Nova Storm begin
causing mayhem at the celebration.
They have a bigger plan for Megatron.
But first they need to drive him
away from his allies.

Megatron quickly begins defending
his allies from his former soldiers.
He fights side by side with
Optimus Prime.

Skywarp and Nova Storm cannot overpower Megatron and Optimus Prime. They quickly fall to the power of the two legends.

Megatron believes that humans fear Autobots because of bots like Skywarp and Nova Storm. He begins to doubt that humans will ever treat Autobots with kindness.

While Optimus Prime and Megatron are distracted, the Decepticons use this as a chance to escape!

Skywarp and Nova Storm create
a new plan to capture Megatron
and bring him back over to
their side.

They pretend to surrender.
With Dot Malto beside him, Megatron
sadly prepares to put his own kind
behind bars.

Megatron and Dot Malto have fallen for Skywarp and Nova Storm's trick! The two Decepticons capture them when they least expect it.
Dot Malto vows to stay by Megatron's side as Skywarp and Nova Storm take Megatron away to their large lair.

The Decepticons direct the Arachnamechs to tie up Dot Malto and Megatron. Megatron tells the Decepticons that he will show them no mercy if they hurt Dot Malto.

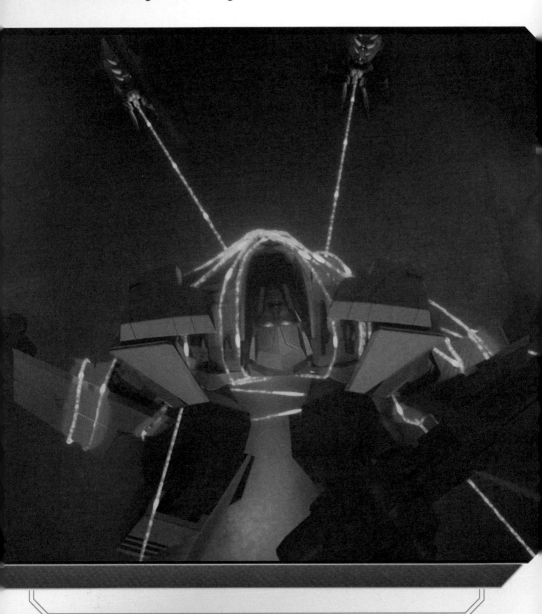

Skywarp and Nova Storm are
shocked by how much Megatron
cares for a human.
They remind him how differently
he once felt about humans.

TRANSFORMERS ATTACK

S&P VIX   23.987 0.53   NASBNK VIX   24.68 0.11   OIL VIX   44   EGN

Skywarp and Nova Storm show Megatron the news reports of their fight with him and Optimus Prime. They tell him that humans will always see Decepticons as evil.

Dot will not let these Decepticons
make Megatron doubt his purpose.
She breaks free and hides in
the large lair.

Skywarp tells Megatron that his only human friend has abandoned him. Megatron wonders if that is true.

In hiding, Dot uses her phone to call
her husband, Alex, and tell him where
they are being held. After Alex tells
Optimus Prime, he and the Malto
children rush to rescue their mom.

In the lair Skywarp and Nova Storm continue to tell Megatron that no one will come to save him.
They try to make him believe his true purpose is fighting alongside them.

Just then Optimus Prime,
his Autobot team, and the rest
of the Malto family
arrive to rescue Megatron!

With the Decepticons distracted,
Dot rushes to Megatron's side
and sets him free.

Megatron pushes his doubts
to the side and begins fighting
alongside his friends.

Skywarp and Nova Storm
are overpowered once again.
This time they will not get away!

Megatron is happy that his friends came to save him, but he questions why G.H.O.S.T. did not show its allegiance to him today.

Optimus Prime says G.H.O.S.T. has work to do, but the Malto family is a team that can be counted on. Megatron looks at the Malto family and is happy. He sees the true Human–Cybertronian alliance!